ROAR-chestra!

A Wild Story of Musical Words

ROBERT HEIDBREDER

Illustrations by DUŠAN PETRIČIĆ

ALLEGRO

Quickly, swiftly — race, run, fly!

ADAGIO

Slowly, smoothly — a steady pace.

GLISSANDO

Gently gliding,
slipping, sliding.

STACCATO

Popping, hopping, bouncing, bounding.

Sweetly twirl,
swirl,
dance,
whirl!

FORTISSIMO

Loudly crashing,
roaring,
stamping!

PIANISSIMO

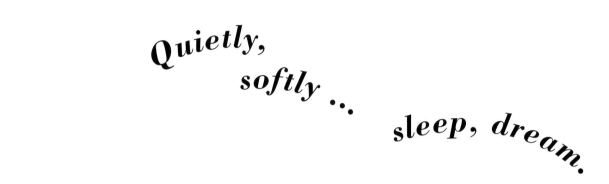

Quietly,
softly ...
sleep, dream.

Shhh ...

The musical terms are in the Italian language because many important early composers were Italian. Here's what the words mean in English:

ALLEGRO [a-LAY-groh]: brisk, lively
ADAGIO [a-DAH-zhee-o]: slowly
GLISSANDO [glih-SAN-do]: gliding, sliding
STACCATO [sta-KAH-toh]: short, detached
DOLCE [DOHL-chay]: sweetly, softly
FORTISSIMO [for-TIH-sih-moh]: loudly
PIANISSIMO [pee-ah-NIH-sih-moh]: quietly

To Sheila Barry, who brought the music of words to so many — R.H.

To Valerie Hussey, my editor and friend, who opened up the blank pages of Canadian children's books for my illustrations twenty-seven years ago — D.P.

Text © 2021 Robert Heidbreder
Illustrations © 2021 Dušan Petričić

Published in Canada and the U.S. by Kids Can Press Ltd.
25 Dockside Drive, Toronto, ON M5A 0B5

Kids Can Press is a Corus Entertainment Inc. company

www.kidscanpress.com

The artwork in this book was rendered in pen and ink and colored in Photoshop.
The text is set in Bodoni.

Edited by Jennifer Stokes
Designed by Andrew Dupuis

Printed and bound in Malaysia in 10/2020 by Tien Wah Press (Pte) Ltd.

CM 21 0 9 8 7 6 5 4 3 2 1

FSC www.fsc.org
MIX
Paper from responsible sources
FSC® C012700

LIBRARY AND ARCHIVES CANADA CATALOGUING IN PUBLICATION

Title: ROAR-chestra! : a wild story of musical words / written by Robert Heidbreder ;
illustrated by Dušan Petričić.
Names: Heidbreder, Robert, author. | Petričić, Dušan, illustrator.
Identifiers: Canadiana 20200300733 | ISBN 9781525302749 (hardcover)
Subjects: LCSH: Music — Terminology — Juvenile literature.
Classification: LCC ML3928 .H45 2021 | DDC j780.1/4 — dc23

Kids Can Press gratefully acknowledges that the land on which our office is located is the traditional territory of many nations, including the Mississaugas of the Credit, the Anishnabeg, the Chippewa, the Haudenosaunee and the Wendat peoples, and is now home to many diverse First Nations, Inuit and Métis peoples.

We thank the Government of Ontario, through Ontario Creates; the Ontario Arts Council; the Canada Council for the Arts; and the Government of Canada for supporting our publishing activity.